Mavis Jukes

LIKE JAKE AND ME

pictures by Lloyd Bloom

Alfred A. Knopf, New York

For my mother and father

—M. J.

85 167

This is a Borzoi Book Published by Alfred A. Knopf, Inc.

Text Copyright © 1984 by Mavis Jukes. Illustrations Copyright © 1984 by Lloyd Bloom.
All rights reserved under International and Pan-American Copyright Conventions.
Published in the United States by Alfred A. Knopf, Inc., New York, and simultaneously in Canada by
Random House of Canada Limited, Toronto. Distributed by Random House, Inc., New York.
Designed by Mimi Harrison 0 9 8 7 6 5 4 3 2
Manufactured in the United States of America

Library of Congress Cataloging in Publication Data
Jukes, Mavis. Like Jake and me. Summary: Alex feels that he does not have much in
common with his stepfather Jake until a fuzzy spider brings them together.
[1. Stepfathers—Fiction. 2. Fathers and sons—Fiction. 3. Spiders—Fiction] I. Bloom, Lloyd, ill. II. Title.
PZ7.J9294Li 1984   [Fic]   83-8380   ISBN 0-394-85608-2   ISBN 0-394-95608-7 (lib. bdg.)

LIKE JAKE AND ME

THE RAIN HAD STOPPED. The sun was setting. There were clouds in the sky the color of smoke. Alex was watching his stepfather, Jake, split wood at the edge of the cypress grove. Somewhere a toad was grunting.

"Jake!" called Alex.

Jake swung the axe, and wood flew into the air.

"Jake!" Alex called again. "Need me?" Alex had a loose tooth in front. He moved it in and out with his tongue.

Jake rested the axe head in the grass and leaned on the handle. "What?" he said. He took off his Stetson hat and wiped his forehead on his jacket sleeve.

Alex cupped his hands around his mouth. "Do . . . you . . . need . . . me . . . to . . . help?" he hollered. Then he tripped over a pumpkin, fell on it, and broke it. A toad flopped away.

Jake adjusted the raven feather behind his hatband. "Better stay there!" he called. He put his hat back on. With powerful arms, he sunk the axe blade into a log. It fell in half.

"Wow," thought Alex. "I'll never be able to do that."

Alex's mother was standing close by, under the pear tree. She was wearing fuzzy woolen leg warmers, a huge knitted coat with pictures of reindeer on the back, and a red scarf with the name *Virginia* on it. "I need you," she said.

Alex stood up, dumped the pumpkin over the fence for the sheep, and went to Virginia.

"I dropped two quarters and a dime in the grass. If I bend down, I may never be able to get up again," she said. Virginia was enormous. She was pregnant with twins, and her belly blocked her view to the ground. "I can't even see where they fell."

"Here!" said Alex. He gave her two quarters. Then he found the dime. He tied her shoe while he was down there.

"Thanks," said Virginia. "I also need you for some advice." She pointed up. "Think it's ready?"

One of the branches of the pear tree had a glass bottle over the end of it. Inside were some twigs and leaves *and* two pears. In the spring, Virginia had pushed the bottle onto the branch, over the blossoms. During the summer, the pears had grown and sweetened inside the bottle. Now they were fat and crowding each other.

The plan was that when the pears were ripe, Virginia would pull the bottle from the tree, leaving the fruit inside. Then she'd fill the bottle with pear nectar and trick her sister, Caroline. Caroline would never guess how Virginia got the pears into the bottle!

"Shall we pick it?" asked Virginia.

"Up to you!" said Alex.

Months ago, Virginia had told him that the pears, and the babies, would be ready in the fall. Alex looked away at the hills. They were dusky gray. There were smudges of yellow poplars on the land. Autumn was here.

Alex fiddled with his tooth. "Mom," he asked, "do you think the twins are brothers or sisters?"

"Maybe both," said Virginia.

"If there's a boy, do you think he'll be like Jake or like me?"

"Maybe like Jake *and* you," said Virginia.

"Like Jake *and* me?" Alex wondered how that could be possible.

"Right," said Virginia.

"Well, anyway," said Alex, "would you like to see something I can do?"

"Of course," she said.

Alex straightened. Gracefully he lifted his arms and rose up on his toes. He looked like a bird about to take off. Then he lowered his arms and crouched. Suddenly he sprang up. He spun once around in midair and landed lightly.

Virginia clapped. "Great!"

Alex did it again, faster. Then again, and again. He whirled and danced around the tree for Virginia. He spun until he was pooped. Jake had put down the axe and was watching.

"Ballet class!" gasped Alex. "Dad signed me up for lessons, remember?"

"Of course I remember," said Virginia. "Go show Jake!"

"No," panted Alex. "Jake isn't the ballet type."

"He might like it," said Virginia. "Go see!"

"Maybe another time," said Alex. He raced across the field to where Jake was loading his arms with logs. "Jake, I'll carry the axe."

"Carry the axe?" Jake shook his head. "I just sharpened that axe."

Alex moved his tooth with his tongue and squinted up at Jake. "I'm careful," he said.

Jake looked over at the sheep nosing the pumpkin. "Maybe another time," he told Alex.

Alex walked beside him as they headed toward the house. The air was so cold Jake was breathing steam. The logs were stacked to his chin.

Virginia stood under the pear tree, watching the sunset. Alex ran past her to open the door.

Jake thundered up the stairs and onto the porch. His boots were covered with moss and dirt. Alex stood in the doorway.

"Watch it!" said Jake. He shoved the door open farther with his shoulder, and Alex backed up against the wall. Jake moved sideways through the door.

"Here, I'll help you stack the wood!" said Alex.

"Watch it!" Jake came down on one knee and set the wood by the side of the woodstove. Then he said kindly, "You've really got to watch it, Alex. I can't see where I'm going with so big a load."

Alex wiggled his tooth with his tongue. "I just wanted to help you," he said. He went to Jake and put his hand on Jake's shoulder. Then he leaned around and looked under his Stetson hat. There was bark in Jake's beard. "You look like a cowboy in the movies."

"I have news for you," said Jake. "I *am* a cowboy. A real one." He unsnapped his jacket. On his belt buckle was a silver longhorn steer. "Or was one." He looked over at Alex.

Alex shoved his tooth forward with his tongue.

"Why don't you just pull out that tooth?" Jake asked him.

"Too chicken," said Alex. He closed his mouth.

"Well, everybody's chicken of something," said Jake. He opened his jacket pocket and took out a wooden match. He chewed on the end of it and looked out the windows behind the stove. He could see Virginia, still standing beneath the tree. Her hands were folded under her belly.

Jake balled up newspaper and broke some sticks. He had giant hands. He filled the woodstove with the wadded paper and the sticks and pushed in a couple of logs.

"Can I light the fire?" Alex asked.

"Maybe another time," said Jake. He struck the match on his rodeo belt buckle. He lit the paper and threw the match into the fire.

Just then Alex noticed that there was a wolf spider on the back of Jake's neck. There were fuzzy babies holding on to her body. "Did you know wolf spiders carry their babies around?" said Alex.

"Says who?" asked Jake.

"My dad," said Alex. He moved his tooth out as far as it would go. "He's an entomologist, remember?"

"I remember," said Jake.

"Dad says they only bite you if you bother them, or if you're squashing them," said Alex. "But still, I never mess with wolf spiders." He pulled his tooth back in with his tongue.

"Is that what he says, huh," said Jake. He jammed another log into the stove, then looked out again at Virginia. She was gazing at the landscape. The hills were fading. The farms were fading. The cypress trees were turning black.

"I think she's pretty," said Alex, looking at the spider.

"I do, too," said Jake, looking at Virginia.

"It's a nice design on her back," said Alex, examining the spider.

"Yep!" said Jake. He admired the reindeer coat, which he'd loaned to Virginia.

"Her belly sure is big!" said Alex.

"It has to be big, to carry the babies," said Jake.

"She's got an awful lot of babies there," said Alex.

Jake laughed. Virginia was shaped something like a pear.

"And boy! Are her legs woolly!" said Alex.

Jake looked at Virginia's leg warmers. "Itchy," said Jake. He rubbed his neck. The spider crawled over his collar.

"She's in your coat!" said Alex. He backed away a step.

"We can share it," said Jake. He liked to see Virginia bundled up. "It's big enough for both of us. She's got to stay warm." Jake stood up.

"You sure are brave," said Alex. "I like wolf spiders, but I wouldn't have let that one into my coat. That's the biggest, hairiest wolf spider I've ever seen."

Jake froze. "Wolf spider! Where?"

"In your coat getting warm," said Alex.

Jake stared at Alex. "What wolf spider?"

"The one we were talking about, with the babies!" said Alex. "And the furry legs."

"Wolf spider!" Jake moaned. "I thought we were talking about Virginia!" He was holding his shoulders up around his ears.

"You never told me you were scared of spiders," said Alex.

"You never asked me," said Jake in a high voice. "Help!"

"How?" asked Alex.

"Get my jacket off!"

Alex took hold of Jake's jacket sleeve as Jake eased his arm out. Cautiously, Alex took the jacket from Jake's shoulders. Alex looked in the coat.

"No spider, Jake," said Alex. "I think she went into your shirt."

"My shirt?" asked Jake. "You think?"

"Maybe," said Alex.

Jake gasped. "Inside? I hope not!"

"Feel anything furry crawling on you?" asked Alex.

"Anything *furry* crawling on me?" Jake shuddered. "No!"

"Try to get your shirt off without squashing her," said Alex. "Remember, we don't want to hurt her. She's a mama."

"With babies," added Jake. *"Eek!"*

"And," said Alex, "she'll bite!"

"Bite? Yes, I know!" said Jake. "Come out on the porch and help me! I don't want her to get loose in the house!"

JONES ELEMENTARY SCHOOL

Jake walked stiffly to the door. Alex opened it. They walked out onto the porch. The sky was thick gray and salmon colored, with blue windows through the clouds.

"Feel anything?" asked Alex.

"Something . . ." said Jake. He unsnapped the snaps on his sleeves, then the ones down the front. He opened his shirt. On his chest was a tattoo of an eagle that was either taking off or landing. He let the shirt drop to the floor.

"No spider, back or front," reported Alex.

They shook out the shirt.

"Maybe your jeans," said Alex. "Maybe she got into your jeans!"

"Not my *jeans!*" said Jake. He quickly undid his rodeo belt.

"Your boots!" said Alex. "First you have to take off your boots!"

"Right!" said Jake. He sat down on the boards. Each boot had a yellow rose and the name *Jake* stitched on the side. "Could you help?" he asked.

"Okay," said Alex. He grappled with one boot and got it off. He checked it. He pulled off and checked the sock. No spider. He tugged on the other boot.

"You've got to pull harder," said Jake, as Alex pulled and struggled. "Harder!"

The boot came off and smacked Alex in the mouth. "Ouch!" Alex put his tongue in the gap. "Knocked my tooth out!" He looked in the boot. "It's in the boot!"

"Yikes!" said Jake.

"Not the spider," said Alex. "My tooth." He rolled it out of the boot and into his hand to examine it.

"Dang," said Jake. "Then hurry up." Alex dropped the tooth back into the boot. Jake climbed out of his jeans and looked down each leg. He hopped on one foot to get the other sock off.

"She won't be in your sock," said Alex. "But maybe—"

"Don't tell me," said Jake. "Not my shorts!"

Alex stared at Jake's shorts. There were pictures of mallard ducks on them. "Your shorts," said Alex.

"I'm afraid to look," said Jake. He thought he felt something creeping just below his belly button.

"Someone's coming!" said Alex. "Quick! Give me your hat! I'll hold it up and you can stand behind it."

"Help!" said Jake in a small voice. He gave Alex the hat and quickly stepped out of his shorts. He brushed himself off in the front.

"Okay in the back," said Alex, peering over the brim of the hat.

Jake turned his shorts inside out, then right side in again. No spider. When he bent over to put them on, he backed into his hat, and the raven feather poked him. Jake howled and jumped up and spun around in midair.

"I didn't know you could do ballet!" said Alex. "You dance like me!"

"I thought I felt the spider!" said Jake. He put on his shorts.

"What on *earth* are you doing?" huffed Virginia. She was standing at the top of the stairs, holding the bottle with the pears inside.

"We're hunting for a spider," said Jake.

"Well!" said Virginia. "I like your hunting outfit. But aren't those *duck*-hunting shorts, and aren't you cold?"

"We're not hunting spiders," explained Jake. "We're hunting *for* a spider."

"A big and hairy one that *bites!*" added Alex.

"A wolf spider!" said Jake, shivering. He had goose bumps.

"Really!" said Virginia. She set the bottle down beside Jake's boot. "Aha!" she cried, spying Alex's tooth inside. "Here's one of the spider's teeth!"

Alex grinned at his mother. He put his tongue where his tooth wasn't.

Jake took his hat from Alex and put it on.

"Hey!" said Virginia.

"What?" said Jake.

"The spider!" she said. "It's on your hat!"

"Help!" said Jake. "Somebody help me!"

Alex sprang up into the air and snatched the hat from Jake's head.

"Look!" said Alex.

"Holy smoke!" said Jake.

There, hiding behind the black feather, was the spider.

Alex tapped the hat brim. The spider dropped to the floor. Then off she swaggered with her fuzzy babies, across the porch and into a crack.

Jake went over to Alex. He knelt down. "Thanks, Alex," said Jake. It was the closest Alex had ever been to the eagle. Jake pressed Alex against its wings. "May I have this dance?" Jake asked.

Ravens were lifting from the blackening fields and calling. The last light had settled in the clouds like pink dust.

Jake stood up holding Alex, and together they looked at Virginia. She was rubbing her belly. "Something is happening here," she told them. "It feels like the twins are beginning to dance."

"Like Jake and me," said Alex. And Jake whirled around the porch with Alex in his arms.

MAVIS JUKES was raised in New City, New York. She was admitted to the California Bar but has abandoned a law career to write. Her first book, *No One Is Going to Nashville,* was published by Knopf in 1983. She lives with her husband, artist Robert Hudson, and her children and stepchildren in Sonoma County, California.

LLOYD BLOOM was raised in New York City. He developed his own technique for painting with pastels while doing the pictures for *Like Jake and Me,* the eighteenth book he has illustrated. He lives in Brooklyn, New York.